KATIE AND HER GRANDMA were in London for the day. When it started to rain Grandma said, "Let's go into the National Gallery and look at the pictures." Katie took Grandma in through a big revolving door, spinning her round and round at least seven times.

Katie had never been to
an art gallery before.
"It's very grand, isn't it?"
she said.
"It is," said Grandma.
"But I need a nice rest after
those spinning doors. You
go and have a look at the
pictures, and be sure to be
back in half an hour . . . "

The first few rooms were full of people, but soon Katie found a room with no one else in it. Katie didn't know which painting to look at first. She stopped in front of a painting of a horse-drawn cart.

*The Hay Wain* by John Constable, she read.
PLEASE DO NOT TOUCH.
"Why not?" said Katie. She slowly reached out
her hand. To her surprise, it went right past the
picture frame and into the painting.
"This isn't a picture at all," cried Katie. "It's real!"
Then, looking carefully around her, she climbed
right into the painting!

Katie looked round in amazement! Then she
set off through the mud to the cottage.

A delicious smell of cooking came from
an open window. Katie found a freshly baked
apple pie cooling on the windowsill, and helped
herself to a large slice. It was so good, she
ate all the rest as well.

"Hey, that was my supper!" yelled a man
on the hay wain. His dog barked, so Katie
thought it might be time to go . . .

She ran back to the
picture frame and climbed
into the gallery.

She peered around the doorway
of the next room. There was a
guard sitting beside the door,
but he was asleep.

Katie went up to the painting she liked best.
*Madame Moitessier* by Jean-Auguste-Dominique
Ingres, she read. PLEASE DO NOT TOUCH.
But, of course . . . she did.

"Hello," said Katie. "What a pretty dress."

"*Merci*!" said Madame Moitessier. "How lovely to have some company. I sit here, being looked at, but no one has ever come inside before. Will you stay for some tea and cakes?"

"Yes, please!" said Katie.

"Now, *un* lump or *deux*?" asked Madame Moitessier, pointing to the sugar bowl.

"*Trois*!" said Katie.

They talked and talked,
and they enjoyed seeing the
surprised faces of the other
visitors to the gallery.
"I haven't laughed so
much for years!" said
Madame Moitessier.
She had to use her fan
to cool herself down.

But Katie laughed so much that she spilt
her tea (it *was* her fourth cup) all over
Madame Moitessier's beautiful dress.
"Oh, how clumsy!" cried
Madame Moitessier.
"Sorry!" said Katie.

She had also managed to get
mud all over the carpet.
She decided to leave before she
caused any more trouble.
She helped herself to another
cake, and jumped out of the
picture and back into the gallery.

Katie wandered into another room,
where she saw a very big painting.

*The Umbrellas* by Pierre-Auguste Renoir, she read.
She noticed a little girl with a hoop in the painting.
'I wonder if she'll play with me?' she thought.
PLEASE DO NOT TOUCH said the notice,
but once again she did.

Inside the picture it was raining.
"Would you like a cake?"
said Katie to the little girl.
"*Merci*," she replied.
"Let's play with my hoop!"
Soon they were having
a wonderful game, bowling
the hoop to each other.

But Katie hit the hoop so hard
it flew right out of the picture!
It bounced on the floor and
disappeared into another
painting. The little girl
began to cry.
"Whoops! Sorry!" said Katie.
She jumped into the gallery and
ran over to the other picture.

It was called *Surprised!* by Henri Rousseau.
Katie saw there was a tiger in the painting.
PLEASE DO NOT TOUCH said the notice,
but she had to find the hoop! So she climbed
over the frame and into the picture.

Katie found herself in a wild jungle.
The wind blew and it was raining
very hard. She was a bit scared of
the tiger, but he ran off through the trees.
Katie couldn't see the hoop anywhere,
so she went after the tiger.

Katie followed the tiger through the jungle.
He led her past a lake full of crocodiles,
that snapped their jaws at her.
But Katie just laughed.

She climbed up a tree and helped herself to a
banana. Just then, she saw the hoop hanging
on a branch.
"Well done, tiger," said Katie, grabbing the hoop.
She followed the tiger back to the picture frame,
and jumped into the gallery.

Katie threw the hoop back into the umbrella picture.
"There you go!" she said.
The little girl was very pleased. They waved goodbye,
and Katie ran off to the next room.

*Exhibition of Modern Art* read Katie. DO NOT TOUCH.

Katie looked at a very different picture.

*Dynamic Suprematism* by Kazimir Malevich,
she read. 'It might be fun to climb up that
big triangle,' she thought.

Without checking to see if anyone was
watching, she jumped inside the painting.

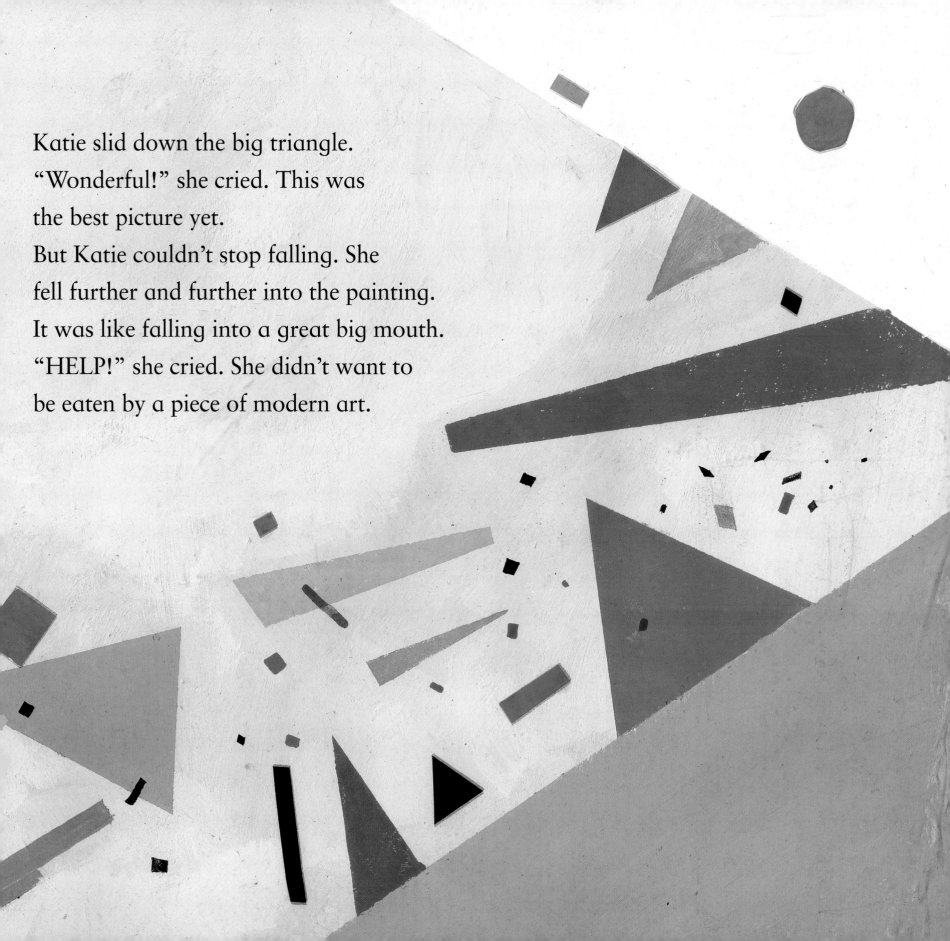

Katie slid down the big triangle.
"Wonderful!" she cried. This was
the best picture yet.
But Katie couldn't stop falling. She
fell further and further into the painting.
It was like falling into a great big mouth.
"HELP!" she cried. She didn't want to
be eaten by a piece of modern art.

Someone shouted, "Hang on!"
It was the guard. He threw a rope
into the painting and Katie grabbed
hold of it. Then he pulled her back
to the picture frame.
"That will teach you to obey
notices," he said.
"Sorry," said Katie. "I don't
think I'll ever do that again . . . "

Katie was covered in
splodges of sticky paint.
After she had cleaned herself
up, Katie thanked the guard
and went to find Grandma.

Grandma was snoozing on a comfy chair.

"There you are," she said, waking up.

"I hope you had a lovely time."

"Yes, thanks," said Katie. "You can see all sorts of wonderful things in paintings . . . "

It had stopped raining now. So, after Katie had bought postcards of her five favourite pictures, they went to find a cup of tea and a piece of cake.

# Get creative with Katie!

I loved my first ever visit to an art gallery –
it was such an adventure! The paintings were all so different
but there was something really special about each one.

Galleries are now my favourite places to visit with
Grandma. I always find a picture that makes me smile,
and sometimes just looking at a painting can
make me want to draw a picture too!

If you go to a gallery, why not take along a
sketchbook and draw the picture you like best?
Maybe one day one of your paintings will be
framed in a gallery too!

*Love Katie x*